SANTA'S WILD GOOSE CHASE
(The Christmas Adventures of Willy and Nilly)

BY GILBERT OSCAR TWYMAN III

illustrations by MEG CUNDIFF

ADDAX PUBLISHING GROUP

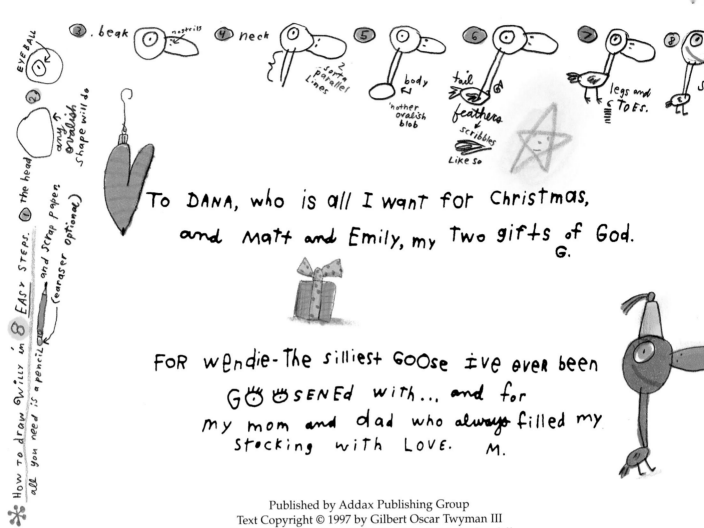

3. beak / nostrils
1. EYEBALL
2. the head — any ovalish shape will do
4. neck — 2 sorta parallel Lines
5. body — 'nother ovalish blob
6. tail feathers & scribbles Like so
7. legs and TOES.
8.

How to draw Gwilly in 8 EASY steps. (all you need is a pencil and Scrap paper) (eraser optional)

To DANA, who is all I want for Christmas, and Matt and Emily, my Two gifts of God.
G.

FOR wendie-The silliest GOOse ive ever been GOOSENEd with... and for my mom and dad who always filled my stocking with LOVE. M.

Published by Addax Publishing Group
Text Copyright © 1997 by Gilbert Oscar Twyman III
Illustrations Copyright © 1997 by Meg Michele Cundiff
Designed by Randy Breeden

For Information address:
Addax Publishing Group
8643 Hauser Drive, Suite 235, Lenexa, KS 66215

ISBN: 1-886110-32-8

Distributed to the trade by Andrews McMeel
4520 Main Street
Kansas City, MO 64111

Printed in the United States of America

1 3 5 7 9 10 8 6 4 2

SANTAS WILD GOOSE CHASE

(THE CHRISTMAS
AdvenTuRES of
WiLLy and NiLLy)

"Now faith is the assurance of things
hoped for, the conviction of things not seen."
Hebrews 11:1

By Gilbert OscaR Twyman III

illustrated by MEG cundiff

Willy and Nilly, the two geese inside the glass, gazed out at all the people passing by.

As always, they were hoping like crazy to talk to some of them.

Willy and Nilly were husband and wife and they lived in a snow globe in a busy department store.

Hundreds of people came by at Christmas time. And Willy and Nilly had a blast, since people were always picking up their snow globe and turning it upside-down. Every time they did, the most wonderful thing happened.

Willy and Nilly were surrounded by a million dancing white snowflakes. Each one wrapped them in a gentle hug, soft and wet as a puppy's kiss.

snow globes
&
globe globes
Aisle ④

gadgets →

ach time the snowflakes danced, so did Willy and Nilly. The snowflakes were so thick you'd have a hard time seeing them. But if you especially loved dancing or if you personally knew a dancing goose, and he or she happened to let you in on the secret that geese dance, then maybe, just maybe, you could see them twirling in there.

"Oops, Sorry dear," Willy would say, because, in truth, he wasn't a very good dancer and often waddled on Nilly's feet.

"That's OK, my Sweet," Nilly would say, kindly. She was no twinkle-toes herself and mushed feathers into Willy's bill doing a tricky duck-under-the-wing move.

"Pardon, darling," Nilly said.

"Nmmmph wormers, Steam bagels," Willy replied through his feather-filled beak.

Nilly knew what he meant: "No worries, Sweet baby."

They smiled tenderly because they adored each other. And they knew you didn't have to be great at a thing like dancing to enjoy it.

Willy especially liked doing the West Coast swing, imagining himself to be Frankie Avalon in an old '60s beach movie.

"Shake a Tail feather!" he hooted.

"Twist and Shout!" Nilly cried back. But she liked it most when they danced beak-to-beak and Willy crooned in her ear,

"Do you love me, do you, Surfer girl?"

"Like the Sun Loves to Set in the West," Nilly murmured.

You may think it strange they weren't singing carols. But Christmas is mostly a time of love, don't forget. So the old surfer-dude songs always brought Willy and Nilly close, even if it was 10-below zero outside.

Sharing each other was about all Willy and Nilly ever wanted for Christmas. You see, geese, when they become boyfriend and girlfriend, promise to stay together for life.

They never break that promise. Because they know, deep inside their warm, downy bodies, that the love they share is their most precious gift.

That's just the way geese are.

But Willy and Nilly did have one secret wish. Every year they wrote the same thing on their Christmas list:

"DEAR SANTA. PLEASE, JUST FOR ONE DAY, LET US FLY OUTSIDE THE GLOBE AND GET TO KNOW PEOPLE BETTER."

As yet, the wish hadn't been granted. But Willy and Nilly never lost faith that it would happen someday. That's just the way geese are. They always believe.

8

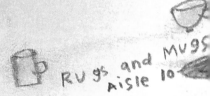

RUgs and MUgs
Aisle 10

*T*hen one Christmas Eve when all the stars God ever created seemed to be out in the wintry sky, a man and woman walked into the store. They stared deeply into the snowglobe and saw two fuzzy bundles inside which, somehow, turned into a tall, handsome man and slender young woman whirling around.

The man and woman were seeing themselves. They had been married 50 years, but now it was as if he and his wife were teenagers inside the globe, skipping the light fandango across the floor.

Whisked away to dreamland, they reached for the globe. Their eyes blurred with tears of joy and they...

... DROPPED iT!
Keee-rash!

The globe broke into a ba-jillion pieces.

EEK!

JT OH

h, I'm so sorry," the woman said, scooping the two geese into her hands.

Then the most amazing thing happened. Willy and Nilly suddenly felt the air rushing under their wings. A surge of power shot through their tail feathers. Their feet began to jitter and their beaks began to twitter.

Before they knew it, they were whooshing up into the lights of the store, whirring about.

"Wheeeee!" shouted Willy, dodging a ceiling fan.

"Man-oh-man, whatta ride!" Nilly cried, loop-de-looping the leather-coat rack.

Everyone in the store was too busy modeling shirts or playing videos or working Swiss Army knife gizmos to see the excited geese.

They swooped down and hovered over the woman's head.

"You just made our Christmas wish come true," said Nilly.

"And you made mine," said the woman. Seeing Willy and Nilly had remind-ed them of their first Christmas together.

With that, Willy and Nilly gave the man and woman tender pecks on each cheek. Then they zoomed out the door as more shoppers plowed in. Willy and Nilly were free!

Swiss Army Knife gadgets

10¢

"What larks!" said Nilly as they climbed into the starry, starry night.

"What a rush!" said Willy, divebombing. "Look at me... I'm Tom Cruise in 'Top Gun.'"

"Hey, Maverick never did that move any better, honey," Nilly screamed.

"Talk to me, Goose," Willy laughed.

"We're lean, mean flying machines," Nilly yelled.

When Willy caught a downdraft and tumbled into a wild ball of feathers, she added, "Uh, slow down a tiny bit, OK, ace?"

But her eyes shone at Willy's antics. And his glowed with pride, too, as he saw Nilly cutting cleanly through the sky.

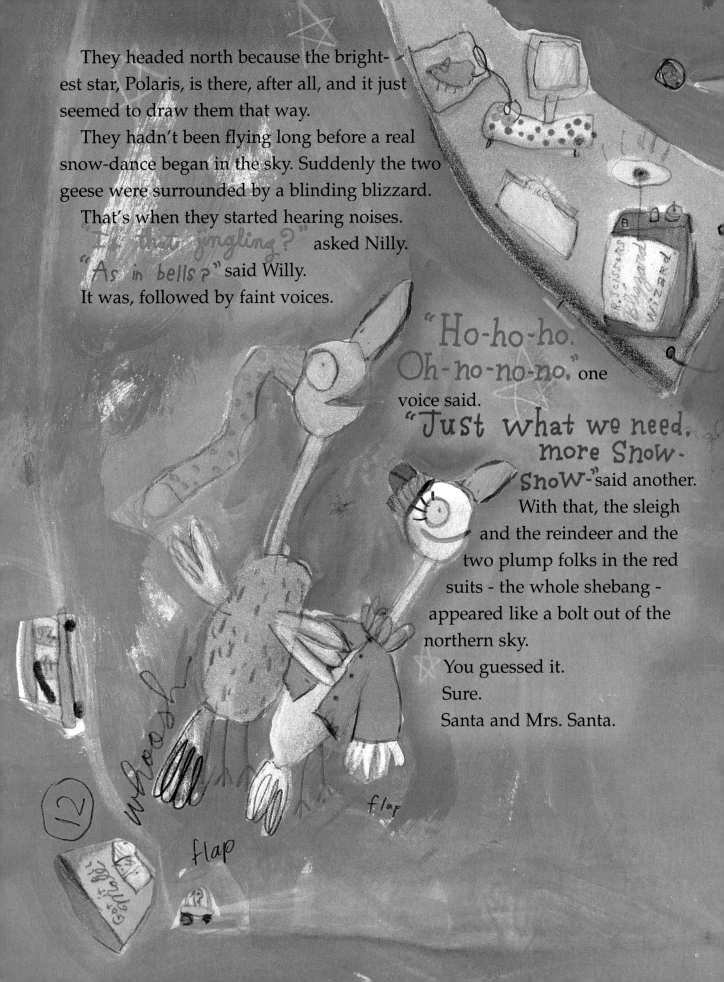

They headed north because the brightest star, Polaris, is there, after all, and it just seemed to draw them that way.

They hadn't been flying long before a real snow-dance began in the sky. Suddenly the two geese were surrounded by a blinding blizzard.

That's when they started hearing noises.

"Is that jingling?" asked Nilly.

"As in bells?" said Willy.

It was, followed by faint voices.

"Ho-ho-ho. Oh-no-no-no." one voice said.

"Just what we need. more Snow-SnoW-" said another.

With that, the sleigh and the reindeer and the two plump folks in the red suits - the whole shebang - appeared like a bolt out of the northern sky.

You guessed it.

Sure.

Santa and Mrs. Santa.

whoosh

flap

flap

flap

⑫

But they did not sound
happy. No, not at all. Not the way you'd
expect on the merriest night of the year.

"I am certain as certain can be that you said,'Turn
left at Rome','" the usually jolly gent was saying.

"Oh good grief," said the normally joyous woman. "I said 'Turn left
at Gnome you know, as in Alaska? Big difference, Big Fella.'"

I am there...

"Tell me about it," said Santa, juggling sandals in one hand and snowshoes in the other. "We just about got this order fouled up."

"As if that would be a first," Mrs. Santa said, rolling her eyes. "When I told you to drop off a **pet rock** for Pat in Pittsburgh, what did you do?"

"I left a **sweat sock**," said Santa. "I was wondering why anyone would want just one."

"And the peanut brittle for Sue in Seattle?"

"I'm afraid I left a **snapping turtle**," admitted Santa. "Good heavens, I hope they don't try to bite into it before it bites into them."

Mrs. Santa was going to say something about her husband getting a hearing-aid when the two geese flew straight into the midst of the Christmas delivery.

Introducing Willy and herself, Nilly asked, "And how are you this wonderful evening."

"Well, bless me if it hasn't been something of a bummer," said Mrs. Santa. "I was just telling Fuzzface here how we were dashing from hither to yon and not getting anything done."

"Well, what about those directions?" said Santa. "Who's in charge of maps?"

He looked at Mrs. Santa, who suddenly looked so sad and tired. True enough, she had the maps and Christmas lists. But they were crumpled in her hands, so soggy she looked like she was holding a heap of snowcones.

"On top of everything else," she said, "I forgot my mittens and..."

"Oh, kitten..." said Santa.

They glanced at the two geese, who were just looking at the squabbling couple, their feathers around each other's shoulders. The sorrowful eyes of the geese seemed to stop the argument in its tracks.

"**S**orry you had to see our spat," said Mrs. Santa.

"Oh, land sakes, that's OK," said Nilly. "Happens to the best of us now and then."

Without another word, she flew to Mrs. Santa and plopped on her hands.

"Your personal handwarmer," Nilly smiled sweetly. The soft down of Nilly's belly soothed Mrs. Santa's reddened hands.

"And your personal umbrella," said Willy, spreading his wings over Santa.

Saying the magic goose-words, **"Ala-quacka-cadabra,"** Willy produced a steaming cup of hot chocolate for Santa.

"Milk from the milky way, chocolate from Mars, where they make the bars, you know? All heated from the sun," grinned Willy.

"I'm on a diet," said Santa.

"From the skim part of the Milky Way," said Willy. "Drink up."

"Ahhhh," Santa said, sipping. His face had been white as the pearly white beard on his face. But now it got rosy, the way Santa's cheeks are supposed to look. His eyes began twinkling. His dimples got merry.

Everyone just sort of perked up.

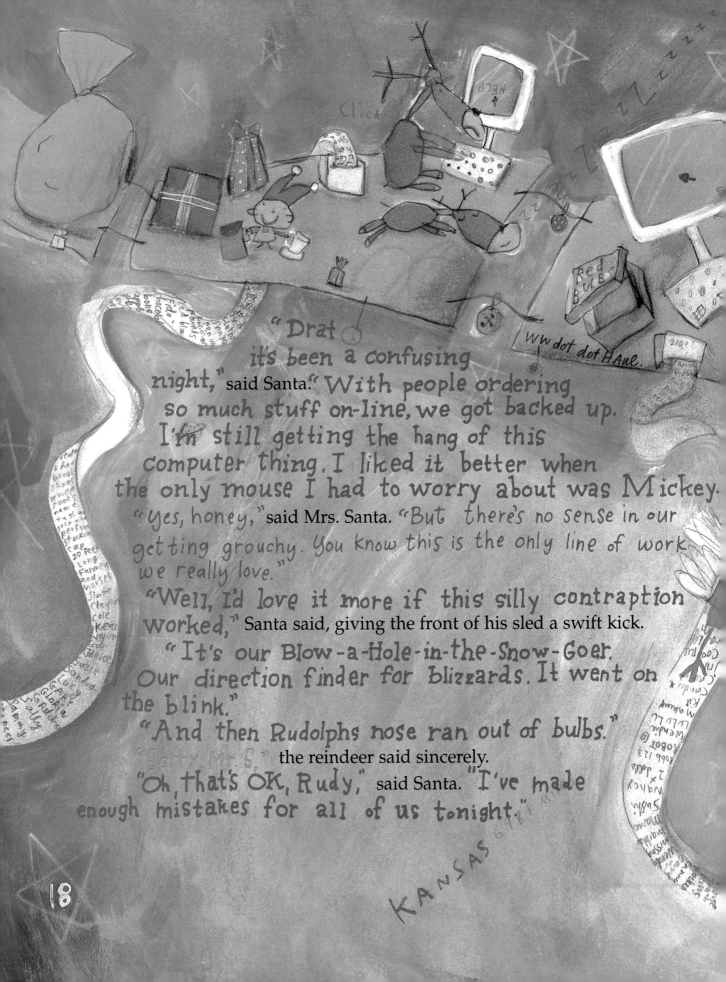

"Drat it's been a confusing night," said Santa. "With people ordering so much stuff on-line, we got backed up. I'm still getting the hang of this computer thing. I liked it better when the only mouse I had to worry about was Mickey."

"Yes, honey," said Mrs. Santa. "But there's no sense in our getting grouchy. You know this is the only line of work we really love."

"Well, I'd love it more if this silly contraption worked," Santa said, giving the front of his sled a swift kick.

"It's our Blow-a-Hole-in-the-Snow-Goer. Our direction finder for blizzards. It went on the blink."

"And then Rudolphs nose ran out of bulbs." the reindeer said sincerely.

"Oh, that's OK, Rudy," said Santa. "I've made enough mistakes for all of us tonight."

18

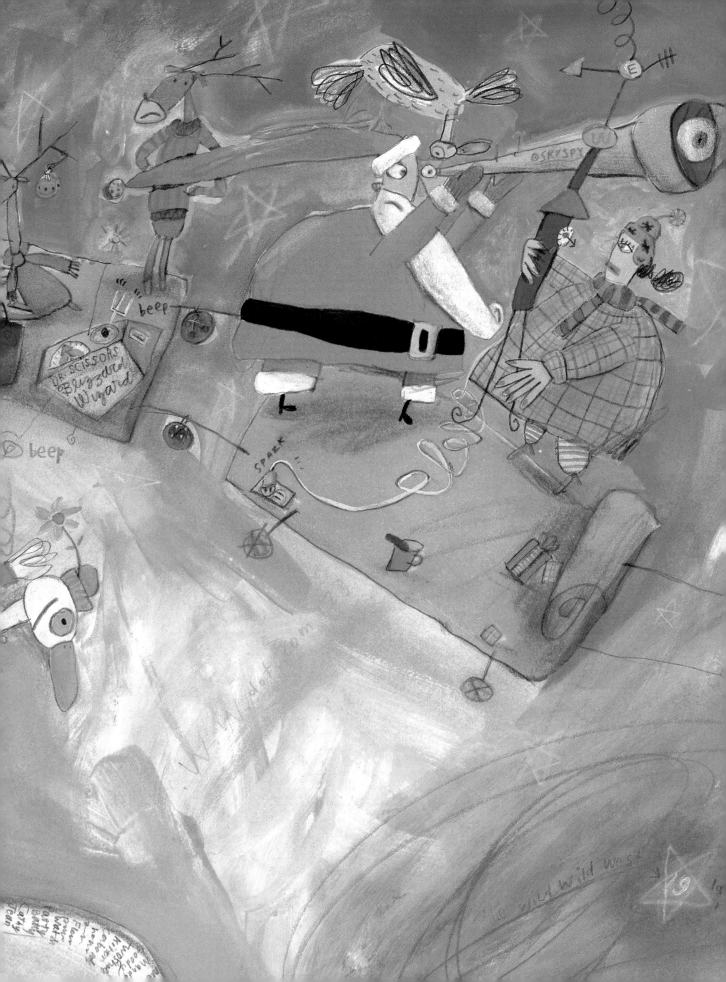

"**E**xcuse me," said Willy. "Let's see if Nilly and I can't help."

The two threw back their long necks and began honking for all they were worth.

Immediately, a dozen geese flew into view.

"You know what to do?" said the head goose, a big, broad-shouldered fellow who introduced himself as Screech.

Willy took one look at the presents needing to arrive before dawn and he felt a surge of strength all the way down to his webby toes.

"You better believe I do, bro," said Willy. "You ready Nilly?"

"I was born ready," she said.

"then let's form up," said Screech—true to his name, screaming into the wind.

In a flash, the geese formed a V. Nilly explained to the Santas that the strongest goose starts at the point of the V, plowing through the wind to make it smoother for the trailing geese. When the lead goose tires, another comes up willingly to take the toughest spot.

"I'll go the first point," said Screech, his deep breaths fairly bursting the down on his chest.

"All right, you jet jockeys. Let's turn and burn!"

He took off in one strong stroke after another.

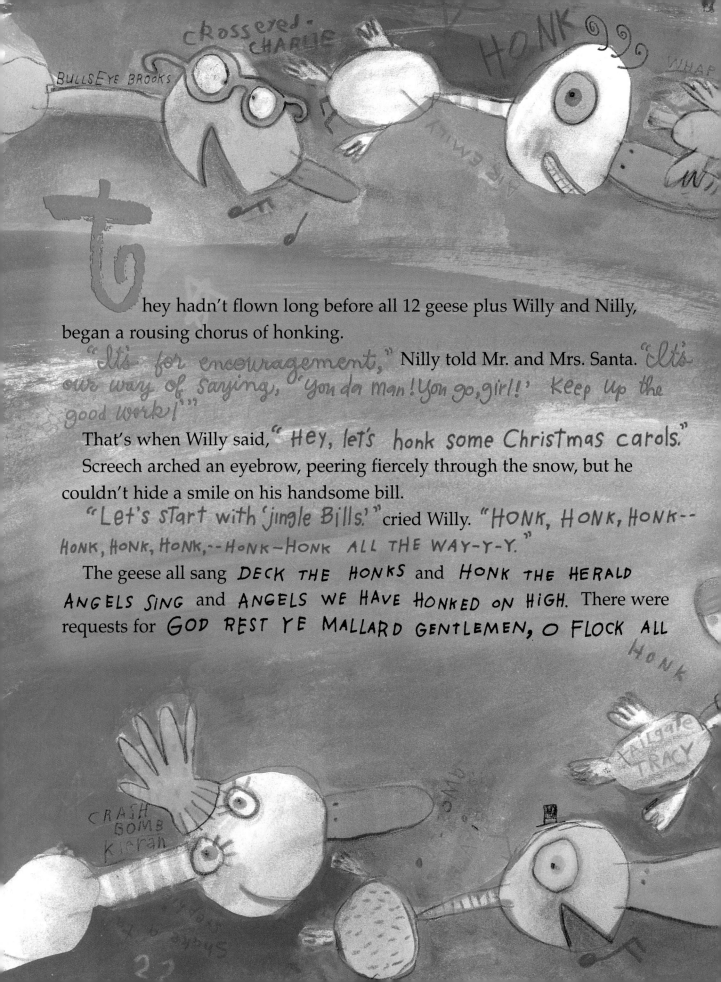

hey hadn't flown long before all 12 geese plus Willy and Nilly, began a rousing chorus of honking.

"It's for encouragement," Nilly told Mr. and Mrs. Santa. "It's our way of saying, 'You da man! You go, girl!' Keep up the good work!"

That's when Willy said, "HEY, let's honk some Christmas carols." Screech arched an eyebrow, peering fiercely through the snow, but he couldn't hide a smile on his handsome bill.

"Let's start with 'Jingle Bills.'" cried Willy. "HONK, HONK, HONK-- HONK, HONK, HONK,--HONK-HONK ALL THE WAY-Y-Y."

The geese all sang DECK THE HONKS and HONK THE HERALD ANGELS SING and ANGELS WE HAVE HONKED ON HIGH. There were requests for GOD REST YE MALLARD GENTLEMEN, O FLOCK ALL

YE FAITHFUL, THE LITTLE DRUMSTICK BOY, O LITTLE DOWN OF BETHLEHEM and WE THREE GEESE. There wasn't a dry eye in the sky when they tenderly harmonized on SILENT HONK, HOLY HONK.

Each goose took a turn leading the V. It turned out Nilly was in the lead when bingo! Just like that, the sleigh popped out of the snowstorm. They were out into the brilliant night with stars winking once again all around.

Screech flew up to Willy and Nilly, his eyes still piercing, but softened with satisfaction.

"We FELT the need..." he said.

"...the need for speed," said Willy and Nilly, laughing.

so you do the ---HOKEY-POKEY

They high-flapped their feathers. They whooped and swooped the sky in a huge S for Santa. They joined wings in a circle and danced the Hokey-Pokey. Don't ask me why. They just felt like it.

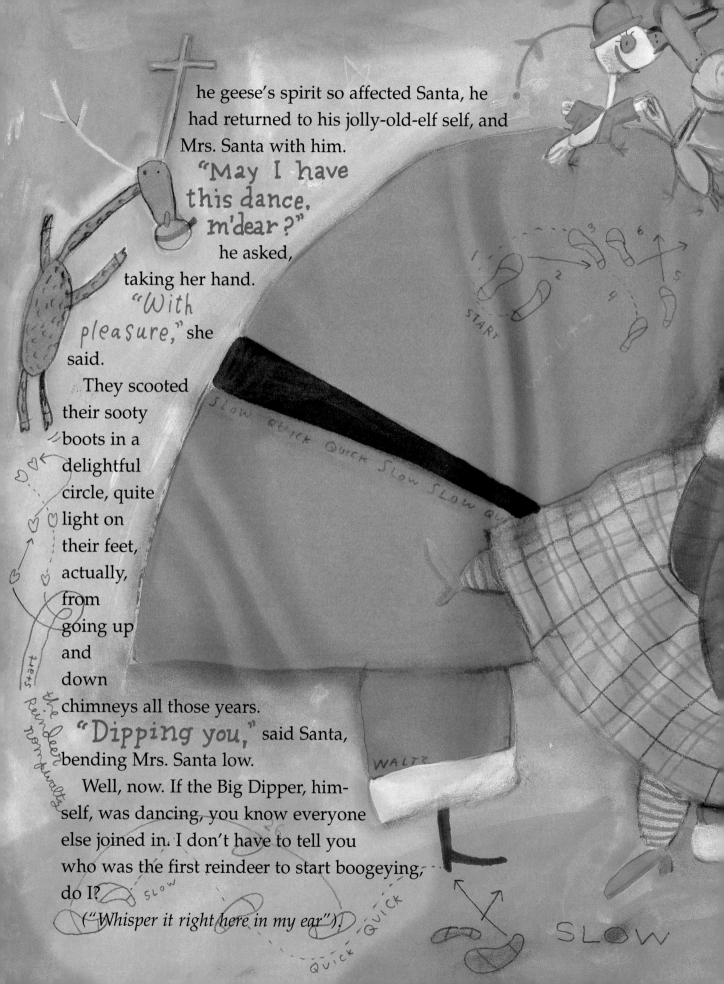

he geese's spirit so affected Santa, he had returned to his jolly-old-elf self, and Mrs. Santa with him.

"May I have this dance, m'dear?" he asked, taking her hand.

"With pleasure," she said.

They scooted their sooty boots in a delightful circle, quite light on their feet, actually, from going up and down chimneys all those years.

"Dipping you," said Santa, bending Mrs. Santa low.

Well, now. If the Big Dipper, himself, was dancing, you know everyone else joined in. I don't have to tell you who was the first reindeer to start boogeying, do I?

("Whisper it right here in my ear").

START

slow quick quick slow slow q

WALTZ

SLOW

QUICK QUICK

SLOW

How smart you are! Of course it was Dancer, who asked Prancer. Dasher danced with Vixen. Comet paired with Cupid and Donner with Blitzen.

Rudolph?

He found a battery pack in Santa's bag.

"I BETTER sit this one out and recharge my nose," he said, sensing his duty. He lent a cheery glow as the Christmas crew shimmied around the sky.

The deer did The Bristol Stomp in honor of England, a Flamenco for Spain, a Minuet for France, a Jig for Ireland and a Polka for Germany. And, of course, a Bunny Hop for their fellow woodland creatures.

Willy and Nilly? They did a ballet duet from Swan Lake, graceful as you please.

*F*inally, Cupid placed two hooves on the Santas shoulders. "So how you two lovebirds doing?" he asked. "Much better, since we ran into those two," they answered, nodding at Willy and Nilly.

With that, Santa clapped his chubby hands and said, "Well, gang, that was some office party. But now it's time to take care of business."

The reindeer hitched themselves to their harnesses. The entire group thanked Screech's Squadron a thousand times over.

"It was our privilege to serve," Screech said with a snappy salute.

"You make us proud," said Nilly.

The Daring Dozen whisked off in formation and banked steep to the right. In an eyeblink they'd changed the V to a C.

"Oh, for Christmas!" said Nilly. "That Screech!"

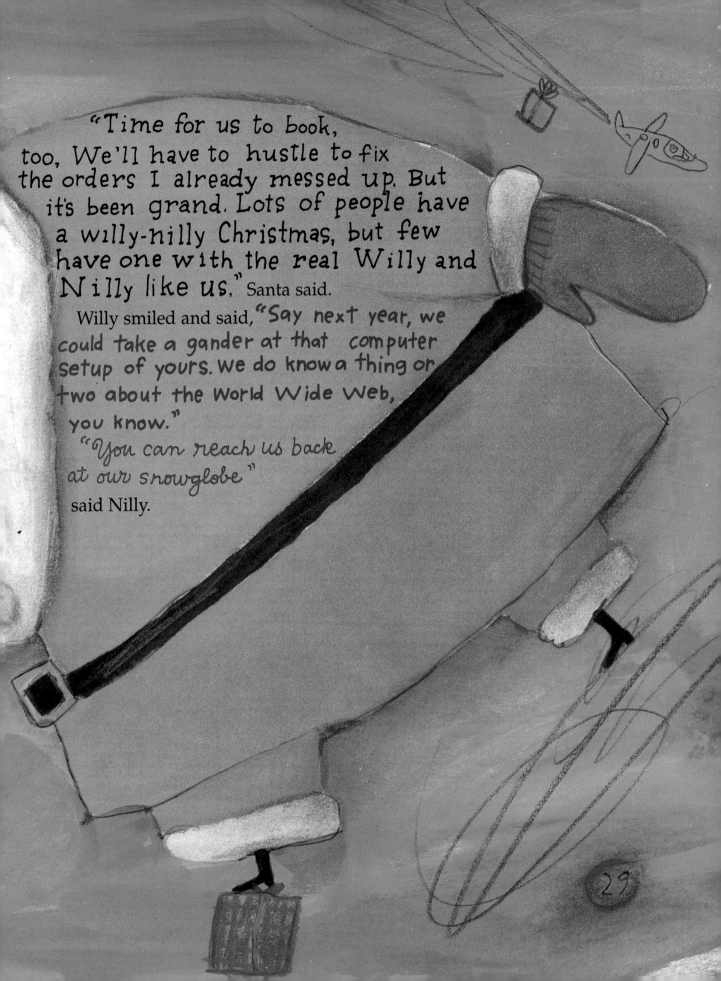

"Time for us to book, too, We'll have to hustle to fix the orders I already messed up. But it's been grand. Lots of people have a willy-nilly Christmas, but few have one with the real Willy and Nilly like us," Santa said.

Willy smiled and said, "Say next year, we could take a gander at that computer setup of yours. We do know a thing or two about the World Wide Web, you know."

"You can reach us back at our snowglobe," said Nilly.

29

"Uh, not so fast," said Santa with a huge smile. "I do have some pull with the real Big Guy upstairs." And laying that famous finger aside of his nose, up out of his sleigh Santa arose.

"I have the honor of telling you," said Santa, "that from now on, your globe will be the actual globe. The entire earth. You are hereby truly free as the other birds. And from now on when you want some snow swirling around you, instead of waiting for someone to pick you up and turn you over, all you have to do is fly to some. They tell me Aspen is pretty nice this time of year."

Willy and Nilly looked stunned.

"But why...how...?"

"Well, you have been praying for this for years, haven't you?" asked Santa.

"Yes," they said as one.

"And of all Gods creatures, as mates for life, are you not some of the best living examples of faithfulness?" asked Mrs. Santa.

"Well..." Willy and Nilly began, modestly.

"Well, then," said Santa. "The way it works, such faith is always rewarded. We just don't always know when or how. Now is your time. This is your time. This is the way."

"We don't know how to repay your kindness," said Willy.

"You already have, just watching yon two," said Mrs. Santa as she and Santa smooched.

The four group-hugged one last time.

"God bless," the Santas said.

"He always does," said the geese.

31

Santa
and Mrs. Santa
sprang back to
their sleigh. To their
team they gave two whistles.
And away they all flew like...well,
since they were really late, it was kind of
like guided missiles.
But before they drove out of sight with
their pack, Willy and Nilly streaked up and
slapped a bumper sticker on the back.
"HONK IF U LOVE CHRISTMAS."
You can do the same whenever you feel like it.
And when you honk, think of Willy and Nilly.

Because with out 'em, our goose
would have been cooked for
Christmas.

The End.